MW00411800

YOUTH IN THE CITY

VARIOUS SMALL FICTIONS

Chris Jalufka

Illustrations by
Thomas Danthony

EVIL TENDER PRESS

YOUTH
IN THE CITY

VARIOUS SMALL FICTIONS

2016 Evil Tender Press
All Rights Reserved

First printing, July 2016.

Illustrations by Thomas Danthony

Book Layout & Design by Ryan Duggan

Printed in Illinois

Illustrations by
Thomas Danthony

CONTENTS

When It's Summer

THE group of children splashed yards off shore. Every few moments a wave would pass, carrying them further out, towards the edge of the world. With each second they gained inches on the horizon.

The children had gone in clueless to what made the Pacific break and sway against the coastal rock. Each face open mouthed, disgusted by the taste of salt-filth, the feel of green water. The sea is not the sterile and pure environment of a suburban swimming pool. Out there under the nameless sky, a humpback's life ends and its corpse becomes the ocean.

The beach was a three-mile stretch of sand that hugged the coast where the homes were painted as Easter candy. This city was elemental. There was the fog and the rush of wind that never stopped. The cliffs and land itself crumbled and we lost footing to the ocean. A flock of kites divided the blue overhead, diving down towards the Earth and back up again to twirl in pointless shapes in the brilliant sky. It was golden daylight and dogs splashed in the wet sand, all sprawl-legged, quick and strong against the patient beating of the ocean, their coats thick with the run off of sweat and ocean froth.

A group of men had taken to the water, desperately paddling, diving against the constant rocking of the waves, to reach the children. I wanted to shout, "They're too far gone. It's over. Let them dissolve."

They're too far-gone to be alive.

The first rush of men pulled the bodies of two young girls ashore. Placed on their backs, side by side, arranged to better understand the situation. One girl was taller only by a matter of inches and both were blonde, their white skin the color of rich butter. They could have been sisters or friends from birth, so much time spent together that they assimilated into one look, one style of female.

A man cried. The others huddled in chatter. With a squint the sun erased the direct knowledge of their bodies and they became light. A fat man bent down to the girls and passed over them with incantations of dead eye contact. He smacked the cheeks of the taller girl then parted her lips and went mouth to mouth, then the other.

The waves moved up the shore washing the foot-prints and all memory of panic. The sand returned to its natural state as a glimmering gel of ocean water. The dogs had gathered around the group begging for attention. Every odd moment a swimmer would break off into the water, shout some incomprehensible word, and let the tide roll them back in, empty handed. From the street two men flanked an elderly woman, walking her through the sand towards the bodies. With each step the two men dragged her along the loose sand with their hands on her back, *"We gotcha,"* guiding her. I stepped aside to let them pass and I asked the man nearest for a cigarette.

"I don't smoke."

The old woman opened her purse and handed me a cigarette.

"I'm out of matches. Sorry."

"I'll find one."

Her face was pale and red, puffed at the eyes from crying but not enough to know how well she knew any of the children, if at all.

The breeze off the water was dry, kissed warm in the sunlight. That arctic chill that made its way across the world was slowly disappearing. I wrapped my sweater around my waist, confident that summer had finally come.

"I've swallowed the voice of reason and now I'm all caw. All communication given through primordial gut speak. Monkey holler and crane shrieks replaced civilized chatter."

Astra

SHE lived in cosmic language. In unknown and haunted mouth speak. In the bedroom she was a blur of oiled hair and blood, milked skin and arms of muscled rope. Fury distilled and made tangible. This wasn't love, no. This was a great and wide-eyed drunkenness on the female existence in general and all of the hallowed places her summer's sweat can pool and dry. This was living, high, inches from death.

After weeks together I woke to find that she had deleted herself from my phone. Pure name removal with all sequences of numbers deleted. A note gave a new address and a new phone number, but the address left behind ended up being an abandoned warehouse and the phone number rang in an echoed void. All I wanted to know was how much time she had spent researching warehouse locations. Had she sought out the perfect venue to act as her final words? Was it supposed to tell me something?

This is me. This is you. Us, together. Left behind. Shattered. Our lives an unwanted and unusable landscape.

"Mothers don't do well with being ignored. Something we all learn rather slowly. The lesson is paid for in long and useless phone calls where the mother rants and you stay put, quietly fuming, pacing a parking lot. Perhaps there are flower delivery costs until the mother is appeased, for now.

Really, the only fun of the relationship is in hearing the mock sacrifice of parenting and its direct likeness to subduing a mythic beast. A child's kiss is really just a Golden Fleece.

I don't know why anyone would want a mother, they seem to do more harm than good."

What We Call Our Own

SHE said she could sing and I believed her. It was easier than having her demonstrate. It was always embarrassing to hear someone sing. Do that thing with their voice that was supposed to entertain and enthrall. Move internal.

From the back of the car she pounded her fists against my headrest, laughing, the sharp points of her heels digging into the vinyl that covered the driver's seat.

"What do you want to hear? I'll sing it. I'll sing that song. Whatever it is."

"You're blurring my vision. I can't see when you do that."

"Focus, motherfucker."

This was a friend of a friend. A lineage that wasn't of any unique pedigree. It was similar to going to the racetrack and reading about the horses. That stream of information that linked foals and mares through distant familial blood. It was supposed to matter. This girl, this friend of a friend, found me through the string of strangers we had in common from years of office jobs in those cities we tried to call home. This was a favor outside of the safe loop of common faces. A simple drive to the airport because she didn't have a car. She didn't have anything. This girl slept on floors and couches of weekend lovers and seasonal friends.

"Why don't you sit in the front seat?"

"My voice will sound better back here. It's called reverb. It's called keeping a spatial distance."

"Is your brother picking you up?" I asked.

"I think so. I got to call him."

"You want to call him now? To make sure?"

"Why are you so worried?"

"I'm not. Just thought I'd ask."

"He knows I'm flying in today. I can't say we really ironed out the details. He's my brother. He'll feel me. Mentally I mean. We don't read minds or anything, we just drop each other clues and then our minds do the work to put the pieces together."

"What does your brother do?"

"He's a courier. He drives around dropping off blue prints and legal forms for a group of contractors and architects. He's connected. His natural instinct is to link divided peoples. His truest quality carried over into his job. He's not separated into halves, day and night, work and play. It all comes from and into the same place. I like that idea."

I could feel her fists massaging up and down the back of my seat, pushing into the material as far as she could, forcing the springs slowly into my back.

"What do you do?"

"I sing."

"Professionally?"

"Of course. If I didn't then it wouldn't be what I do."

She rolled down the window and with her face in the wind, she began to sing. Inside that steady pulse of accelerated breeze her voice was silenced, a distant muffled shout inches from my ear. Her face rippled against the wind. Distorted. Mouth agape bellowing into the tuneless hum of freeway static.

She was a pretty girl. If she wasn't she'd be taking the bus. There is a need for that classic role of the man that fawns over a beautiful face, falling secretly in love with a girl he will never have. I was doing my part. At a distance she made a decent object for affection, at least for a while. She was here to act as an event that could be used in case I felt something for someone in the future and needed a point of reference. I could always tell myself, *"Remember driving that girl to the airport? See? You have made attempts to be close to someone."*

"If you're lucky enough to be drunk when you fall asleep, the sky giants grant you magnificent dreams."

Common Static

DREAMS start as sparks, and then someone dies, always, in dreams. The phone rang and we talk. What we talk about are his dreams. Not dreams as in heartfelt fantasy, but what he watches in his shut eyed coma-state.

He tells me he's on. 'On' like a television is on. A radio. Human broadcast. "There is no future when you sleep," he tells me. "You only see what has happened in the past, but just the worst of it, and you see that shit over and over," he says. "Mine is getting caught in the fifth grade by Jeanine Wilburt on the trail to school. I was walking home and had to shit. I dropped my pants and leaned against a tree, you know, like I'm sitting on a bar stool, and went. In this dream I see Jeanine's stupid fucking face watching poop fall from my ass."

Propulsive shame memory. An event on re-peat deep in the recesses of your heart. The mind has one free second and there it is, Jeanine's face. She sees you again. There's no clenching or cut-ting off now so the shit falls down the bark of an oak tree. You find yourself deep in gut-panic. Burning up from the inside. The world needs to leave you alone, but it won't. The ceaseless flow of embarrassing memories can leave your stomach a mess, knotted and pricked.

"I drink myself to sleep. Ambien helps. Fucking classic dead sleep. Nothing finds you then. Nothing, man."

Sleep is darkness and mimics death. Dreams come and true life rings in as anxious nightmares. My friend struggles to sleep and when sleep does come it's an all night terror. This is what we talk about. Our common ailment. There is a beginning to sleep. A change in your internal weather as you prepare to stop the work of day living. You change clothes and lie on your back in the black and wait for your thoughts to disappear. This is where the troubles lay, in mid-float.

Sleep won't come because I'm afraid my insides will erupt, not as a heart attack, but in absolute body explosion. I can feel it coming. My father had a stroke a few years ago and now it is my turn. Every night I can feel it coming. Waiting to slow me down.

So I play a game. I imagine a closed theater curtain with a word scrawled across it. Spot lit. First it reads *"vehicle"* and the words change like slides in a presentation. The words continue, *"...car, train, bike, plane, shoes..."* The brain focuses on these words and I forget about my potential death. The curtain changes and I lose track, so now I'm in junior high trying to flirt with a girl that, I later learned, never liked me. I stutter and ramble, reach for her hand. I don't remember why. The embarrassment and shame hit like they'd never left. My chest stiffens and I can't move my left shoulder.

I bring back the curtain but this time it's all soft and forgiving numbers, "...*five, fifteen, twenty, twenty five, thirty...*" The numbers sputter across like an old black and white film. A man rides a bike; a horse trots. Twenty-four frames per second slowed down to a sleep-inducing hymn.

I get a call the next day. We talk about our lack of sleep and the anxiety, but not the cause. There is no talk of where it comes from. It's hard enough reliving shame, regret, disappointment, and embarrassment in a night-filled empty room, but these things do not need to be spoken of during the light of day. Something is going to get us, each one, and it will most likely start at the heart. It is an engine and a muscle. It pumps because it remembers to, but it remembers other things as well. It can recall every second of its life, and with little prompting can take you back to places you never want to see again.

Columbus & Broadway

SOME called her "Doodie" and others "Dots." Most of us, those that knew her, just shouted "Dorothy!" when her breasts came out beneath the colored lights of The Casbah. She was the only girl there who bothered to dance, who truly performed. She traded in her sexuality for athleticism – her routine was full of twirls and bends with moments of flamenco inspired high-leg lifted foot stomps and arched back moves, her face stern with false yearning. That one always got a laugh from the crowd.

The scattered voices in the dark would shout, *"Doodie drops!"* and she would leap onto the brass pole and hold herself erect, her arms strong and her body stiff, levitating two feet from the floor. Her legs would lift into the splits and Dorothy could hold that pose for minutes, all reference to the rhythm of the music gone. We shared in that pause, the crowd mirrored across the neon darkness of the club. The tension dissolved once Dorothy released her grip on the pole and dropped, her legs in that floated split, just as she was to hit the ground she would grip the pole once again and come to a complete stop like a televised car crash put on freeze frame before anything bad could happen.

The voices bellowed and barked, and a *"Let's hear it for Dots!"* would shout from some obscene voice within the walls. The crowd drifted off, each man traced the room for a girl willing to bounce topless on his lap for a few minutes in a coffined box, while the steady drone of drumbeats erased all reason to talk. Dorothy would pace the room of men and if there were no buyers for a dance, she'd get out of the club through the side door and wait until her next time on the stage. There she'd be, not on the street but up in the alley, covered in a heavy pea coat and wool cap.

"Did you need a cigarette?"

"Need?"

"Want a cigarette."

"No thanks. I'd rather die slowly, the natural way."

"They're not bad for you. Not anymore."

"Who told you that?"

"I heard it on the news."

"You shouldn't trust the voices of people you don't know." She spoke with a monotone husk. A leathered and rustic rumble. "If you want a private dance, I'll be back on in an hour."

"Are you a gymnast?"

"Did you hear me?"

"I'm just talking."

Dorothy was an attractive girl, perhaps beautiful.

I'm not sure. Her body, all the skin and bones of it, was tight and stiff. The frame of a young twenty-something raised somewhere healthy where the sun beat down harsh and violent. She had no trace of the city in her.

The other Casbah girls worked their sexuality, it was escalated. Dorothy created another form of falsehood. She tried to be better than you.

"Good response in there."

"They laughed. They always do."

She could smile when she wanted to and it was a wide, brilliant smile; all white horse teeth, perfect in size and shape. Her nose dipped low and ended in a small marble that could touch the deep red of her puffed lips. There was blood of Eastern Europe in that nose and the bright green of Ireland in her eyes.

After her second turn on the pole only a few dollars rested on the edge of the stage. She walked the floor offering private dances. She was as naked as the other girls but her body didn't strut or stroll. She didn't glide like them, she moved like something more industrial; a crane or an ocean liner carrying cargo, there was purpose to what she did but it wasn't clear what she was building.

We walked the streets together, hoping to find a diner that was open late. We headed towards the water and the Golden Gate Bridge. A cover of fog wet our faces and coats, and in the mist the street-lights gauzed the world, the trees and storefronts fell ghost-like.

"There's a pizza place around the corner. By the slice."
I bought her dinner and then we walked, mostly in silence with the occasional, "hold up" or "this way."

The air was crisp and damp and she marched on, pea coat buttoned high and her wool cap tugged below her brow. Her cheeks glowed pink and her lips shrunk down in the cold. Water crested at her eyes yet she didn't complain and there were no comments about the weather.

Dorothy's pathways were into the hidden city. She lead me through a series of alleys and shortcuts that lead to the unlocked service door, ironed deep into the building's brick facade. The room was a narrow cave, its ceiling of water pipes twisted and curved overhead, each one painted black like the ceiling they were riveted into. A wooden bar stretched the distance of the room, a barman stood behind, hundreds of bottles at his ready. The floor sloped and we were submerged below the city, beneath what must have been a hotel or a hospital. The barman brought us two glasses of scotch and took my twenty-dollar bill and walked off.

"The man likes to tip himself I guess."

"It's past three in the morning. He can do whatever he wants."

Dorothy removed her wool cap, her hair flattened with rain and sweat. She kept her coat on, which ran the length of her body, ending just below her bare knees. Her blue sneakers had turned black from the slow rain and puddles in the streets. Her bones loosened beneath the fight of muscle and she sat limp in her chair.

"How many times do you think you've seen my tits?"

"Eight times. At the most."

I can tell you all of this because I knew her and we did spend this time together. Dorothy, Doodie to some, rolled out of her seat and I followed the stumbling swerve of a brilliant woman, the back of her pea coat lifted, clinging to the concave swoop of her lower back. She ran into a wall, held herself straight, and stroked her coat back flat. She turned to face me, her coat tousled at the neck, the flap of collar high up at her ears.

"I appreciate the fact that you can keep your mouth shut for a good portion of the evening."

It was then that I knew she was drunk.

We walked and the blackness was beginning to lift to the morning, but not yet. The taxis, buses, and cars had disappeared and we were the only movement on the city's streets. Her drunk was deep and her consistent march was now a hard won stumble. At the first dull pink of morning we were at the gate of her building.

"Want a drink?"

"Sure."

"There's a couch in there. I'll grab some beers." Dorothy drank and unbuttoned her coat. Her eyes twitched in the binary code of the fitfully sloshed. The hours pulled us to sleep but the light, the sun and the day, wanted us awake so we fought.

"I have no idea where I am."

"Does it matter?"

Morning went on and we drank. By the time the sun had finally broken into the sky we were both asleep. It was hours of pure black dream-less sleep and nocturnal headache. When I finally woke Dorothy was still crumpled on the couch. I let myself out and wandered home, finding a taxi along the main street that ran along side the park.

I did pay for sex with her once, I had to. It was before this night but it was the first of many. I followed her home and we drank, and she told me how everyone laughed and I hadn't. She needed money but didn't want me to just give it to her. It was a fair trade but the next time at The Casbah the evening repeated and I got the sex without paying. A few more evenings and the sex disappeared. As time went on I drank all the beer I could and Dorothy would pass out earlier and earlier. She used to be able to go for three days straight on tacos, alcohol, and lazy fucking. Now she couldn't even make it to noon the next day.

Years passed and she forgot my name. At night I recall the shape of her breasts and the damp wool air of her apartment and I'm young again.

Vodka Tonic

HE asked how babies were made, as a joke in a crowded bar. He wanted to hear the words associated with the task; the dry obscenities over the open public air. At the table were fifteen friends, associates, and familiar faces he'd seen every Monday through Friday for the past five years.

"That girl over there," he thought, "I want to hear her say vagina."

No one offered him an answer.

Perhaps they didn't know how babies were made, the biology of it. All they could mutter would be terse words, "Sex." "Fucking." Beyond that, knowledge of blood and seed were non-existent. Babies weren't made, they thought. They come forth and tear themselves into the world as a bag of bones, a creature both holy and monstrous. Birth was the disaster of sex and boredom that resulted in a leash of flesh and the wet voiced piece of you and of another.

His question rested inside of them. They were getting older. Aged past their prime and kids still scared them. Drinking was easier than explaining children. He needed someone to play along and stand up to the task of being obscene in the dead space of the bar. All he wanted was a few words, brief descriptions of love in action and the parasitic by product. He needed to know he wasn't the only one who knew it existed.

"We drink like savages with fists of water, but the water burns and the fists are pints. There is a constant dimness as the windows are blacked out by grease and tar. Someone hugs me and yells, "Francis was a good man..." I agree and he falls in my arms. He huffs into the folds of my sweater, laughter and tears. Pain and joy.

It's all here in the crowd and we live like gutted beasts, covered in the self-blood and shock of what being alive has become."

Value Drops as Soon as You Leave the Lot

ON her refrigerator was a small photograph that she had taken of herself years ago in the bathroom stall of a neighborhood pub. Cramped and sitting down, you can make out a blurred shape on her lap arching like a small bridge from leg to leg.

"Who's that?"

"Me."

"No, on your lap."

"That's my purse. Just a stupid thing. I wasn't really going to the bathroom."

"It looks like a head resting...by your stuff."

"Jealous?"

In the photograph her hair is bright pink, clipped down with children's barrettes. Her eyes shrunken behind a pair of chunky black frames. The white fringe of her navy blue dress frayed. It appears as a costume, unreal. A girl imagined as a cartoon of

the elderly. A young body buried under grandma's
Sunday best.

"Is your roommate out?"

"I don't have one. Just me here."

"You're the first person I've met here without a
roommate."

"It gets lonely."

The apartment was furnished in pale woods and
sanded steel. The walls bare but for a single family portrait placed on the bookshelf. Two older
brothers. Her father, athletic. She's her mother in
miniature.

"All I have is white wine. Chardonnay. I usu-
ally keep a bottle of merlot, but my parents were in
town last weekend."

"Whatever you have is good."

"Not a big wine drinker?"

"Maybe a bottle from 7-Eleven if I think
about it."

"They have wine there?"

"Yeah, next to the cat food."

She disappeared into her bedroom, and when
she came back she had changed out of her office

gear into a pair of pajama bottoms and an over-
sized college sweatshirt. After we ate I loaded the
dishwasher. Something was on television about a
business somewhere that offered its service in pet
portraiture. Bring your cat or dog in, and they can
dress it up and set it against a hazy blue back-
ground and snap — fifteen wallet sized photos
and a large print for your home.

"I'd love a picture of my cat in a little pumpkin
costume. With a tiny pumpkin stem hat on."
She had curled into the arm of the couch, sip-
ping wine from her coffee mug. I didn't know
why I was there, perhaps as an accessory. A
person to fill the other chair at dinner. Her in
pajamas while I'm still dressed from a day's work,
some aspect of civility was missing. I had gone
from potential mate to brother in the course of
one night. I was no threat and no treasure. We
had met a few days earlier in the bedroom of a
shared neighbor and made plans to meet again.
I enjoyed her company. She was pleasant and
smiled a good amount. This was enough.

"Are you going to bed?"
"No, why?"

"The pajamas."

"I'm sorry, do you mind? I didn't think we would be going anywhere tonight."

"Do what you got to do. I just feel a bit over dressed."

"Hold on, I'm going to get something from my room."

Gender wasn't supposed to matter in friendship, that system of cordial talking and laughing was based on the internal, but to imagine her body bare was instinct. To weigh my desire to kiss her used an archaic inner scale. It was a minimal desire, but it was there solely based on her being a woman. She fit my generic want.

"Look."

It was a photo album of a trip to Australia. Snapshots of strangers surfing and scuba diving, her hiking and smiling with people I didn't know. It was a trip looking for large fish and one day she hoped, she would see a great white shark.

At the door I put on my jacket and stepped to the stair well. She hung back at the door, saying something, her arms pressed against the wooden

frame. I walked down the blocks, heading home.
From the hill where she lived you were eye level to
the end of the ocean, the black from the sky falling
into the water. Only the distant lights of the cargo
ships drew the line of the horizon.

At the corner store I picked up a loaf of
bread, a brick of cheese, and a bottle of four dol-
lar wine. By time I got home it was midnight and
I gave her a call to say whatever came to mind
first. The phone rang and I left a message. I hit
start on the DVD player and watched whatever
had kept me awake the night before.

The next day there was no message from her, and
in fact, there never would be.

"What happens in empty space? I dunno. You're just there. That's it. That's the point. Floating, but not in water but in something else. Sand. I don't know. Wind maybe. In a wash of ash and stardust, dead black sight and rolling, topsy turvy and then - bam. You're cut loose from a point where you thought you were already lost. And that's life. But with bills and rent to pay and obligations you can't explain. Yeah. That's life."

All Knowledge
is Accounted For

HE hadn't worked in months. That was all right since he had television. There was still enough in the bank so his rent was paid and time passed in segmented ticks of sitcoms, dramas, and cooking shows.

At the start of summer he received an offer for a customer service position at the headquarters of a telecommunications company. His hours would be spent being a faceless company ear for customer complaints. June wasn't in any position to be picky. This was a step up from working at the gas station and his parents might be impressed that he had a job that was indoors working for a company that they had heard of. On his first day he was guided to the interiors room, a warehouse of cabled walls and satellite mock-ups. This is where the main signal spoke. June's workspace housed the interference monitor, a lone computer that's only function was to blink when the main satellite lost signal with its siblings and ground control.

"Take a seat."

"Then what?"

"Watch the monitor. If Pasha has issues, the monitor blinks."

"Pasha?"

"The satellite. They named her." The boy smiled.

June said, "I was told I was here to answer phones. Billing questions and stuff like that."

"You're here for Pasha. We have a team of sibling satellites, but she's the real deal. They all speak to each other, but she is the only one that speaks to us. She lets us know what parts of the country have weak or no cell reception. Pasha passes along phone calls, text messages and other Generic Civilian Data. GCD. That's what we call it. Pure useless data."

"Just sit and watch?"

"Pretty much. If you have any questions, which you shouldn't, pick up the phone and ask for Phil. There's only one."

"One phone?"

"One Phil. Feel free to bring a book."

June had the graveyard shift. It was spent drinking coffee and staring at the monitor, waiting for Pasha to speak to him. He was paid decent enough and sequestered away from people, so he was happy. It was company policy to not have machines police each other. In order to guarantee that there were no failures in the system they would need a never-ending chain of electronic eyes turned on each other. That was too expensive so they opted for human surveillance. The other benefit of human to machine contact was, if at some point there was a failure, they could simply call it a "human error."

The walls of the interiors room were tiled with rack-mounted patch bays. Floor to ceiling lengths of paneling, black and pock marked with eighth inch silver lipped inputs, from each dangled colored cables in taut arcs, connecting machine to machine. The interference monitor was on a plain desk covered in a skin of false wood where June sat, motionless.

His first week at the company ended and his parents took him out for a celebratory dinner. He had found a job, finally. They had it in their heads that their son was brilliant, and somewhere inside of him was a genius that just had not been found. He didn't finish college and they told him it was okay, plenty of successful people didn't have college degrees.

"Here, we got you a present." His mother handed him a small box. Inside was a medallion depicting a man trudging through a mountain range, walking staff held high.

"It's Saint Christopher. The saint of travelers, those on a journey. This job is the start of your own great adventure."

"Thanks."

They glowed and he didn't want to tell them that all he did was watch a screen. They were proud and that was enough. June walked his parents to their car and watched as they drove off, disappearing into the city. He went back into the restaurant and ordered a beer. In two hours he was drunk and left his car behind, walking the four miles back to his apartment.

June was routinely checked on by a man built of fat and latticed muscle. A few inches short of being a giant. They called him Canary, an interspatial transient, moving from one department to the next. He had designed and developed all of the satellites that were currently in orbit and it was his job to check on them and those that watched over the darkened sky.

"What's going on in the world, June?"

"She's still black."

"Good."

"What if I do get a blink?"

"You call me."

"And?"

"And I get on my gear and calm her down. That's not your worry though, so just make sure you have my number ready when the time comes."

"Comes for what?"

"You'll know."

"What if I get bored?"

"Bring a book."

"That's what Phil said."

"Do you know what all of this is, June? In the Earth's surface-skin are millions of strands of fiber optic cables, relaying our speech and thoughts from home to home, into the atmosphere, deeper, into the far distant yawn of space. Above us all are the satellites, twisting and ringing with the ghost voice of American chatter. I dare you to get bored. It's goddamn Disneyland in here."

During the day shifts Canary would stop in more frequently. June's office was tucked away from the rest of the workers, so he knew that Canary had to make a special trip each time he checked in on him.

"We all good, June?"

Canary kept a gentle sway, a mountain moved by breeze. This was how he slept. In flashes. A few shut-eyed moments in the shower while his hair conditioner set. Sudden REM sleep waiting at a red light. He had spent too much of his life creating machines to consciously remember what he needed to do to be alive, so something inside of him took over and he survived on muscle memory.

"You okay?"

"Just sleeping."

"Doesn't look like it."

"Good. I don't want you to be able to tell. I'm a scientist. All brain-thought. Pure totemic ritual."
"Sounds fun."

"Listen to me, June. I know it gets difficult to sit here. I do. Don't let it get to you. I really want you to work out, hear me?"

"Thanks, I'm good."

"That's good to hear. If you ever have any problems let me know. Like I said, I want you to work out."

Food options consisted of a row of vending machines back at the main lobby of the building. Customers stood in staggered lines, hands full of problematic bills and out of date cell phones.

When calling customer service didn't help, users would show up with the hope that a face-to-face discussion would solve their issues. A soft heat rolled through him and June felt a quick panic build. He covered the company logo on his polo shirt and dropped his quarters into the vending machine.

"Hey, don't worry. They don't risk losing their place line to talk to us over here." A young man held his hand out. June shook it, keeping his other hand over the logo. The boy's smile fell, he leaned in close for whisper.

"You work with Carneros?"

"Canary."

"Yeah, that's him. Gave himself that nickname from what I hear. I heard he hated having a Hispanic name, thought he wouldn't be taken seriously." The boy filled his pockets with candy bars and packs of mints. Fisted two cans of soda and tucked bags of chips under his arms.

"Is he taken seriously?"

"This company exists because of him, so yeah, he's taken seriously. Still, be careful. Carneros keeps one assistant who always seems to end up being here one day and gone the next. No one knows what happens to them, or they just don't want to tell us. The company pulls some kid from

the phone pool and throws them to Carneros
and it happens again. Jeremy lasted almost a year.
That's a good run."

"I never made it to the phone pool."

"No offense. I was offered the job when I first
started but turned it down. Most of us on the
floor do."

June chalked it up to rumor mongering, something that did not interest him at all. He didn't
care for people, and he cared even less about what
they thought about.

Canary held his eyes on the monitor. He connected the screen to Pasha, invisible, high above. This
was her only voice and she rarely spoke, although
she was not an unwilling conversationalist. The
satellite sent back a steady flood of information
for Canary to pore over and had since his team
first designed her.

"I can take over now," June said.
Canary had lost himself and forgotten his physi-
cal form at the moment. He sat open mouthed,
drool repelling from his lips onto his shirt.

"What happened to Jeremy?"

"Why are you asking me that?"

"Some kid on the floor says he disappeared."

"Nope. Just left. Don't listen to them. Listen

to me. Sit here, do your job and don't worry about anything beyond that."

After Canary left June scoured the room. He didn't know what he was looking for but he knew the point was to look anyway. The patch bays were mounted to the walls and left no space for anything else. His search was done in a matter of minutes. He had a desk, a garbage can full of broken pencils and candy wrappers, and a telephone. June picked it up and an interiors operator answered. He asked for Phil.

June walked with Phil on his rounds. Phil, as a prefect, was an administrative assistant to the entire interiors department. This meant he dealt with internal documents, unloaded shipments, and did all other random jobs that needed to be done.

Getting bored, are you?" Phil smiled to himself as June followed him down the hall."

"All I do is sit there. I can see why all of Canary's assistants leave."

"Can you?"

"Yeah. It can drive a guy nuts."

"What have you heard?"

"Nothing."

"What is it? I know those guys out there.

They talk."

"Just said that Canary's assistants disappear, that's it. They don't know why."

"Listen. What we do here is simple enough. A phone company. Nothing special. But think about it this way, we have a bunch of satellites orbiting Earth, their sole job is to pass our data around. The thing is, they do this constantly and the by-product of them having the ability to gather and relay information is that they also gather and relay information that isn't ours. Imagine you're a farmer and need dirt to plant your vegetables. There's not enough so you start digging up a hill for more dirt, but as you dig you find gold. All you wanted was dirt, but the by-product is a fucking treasure. Every inch of space has been accounted for. Jeremy and the others found out, and that's that."

"What'd they find out? What's out there?"

"Only Canary really knows and that's fine with me. I don't want to know."
June headed back to his desk. He was curious now, and he hated that. It was better when it was just a job and there was nothing to think about. He liked not having to think. June dozed off, startled back to life by the phone. It was Canary.

"How's everything, June?" He could let it go,

forget what Phil had told him. It would be easy. Just ignore his questions and say goodbye and hang up.

"What happened to all of your assistants?"

"They left."

"Phil told me they found something out."

"I took you for someone like me. Someone who didn't care."

"I want to know. What happened to Jeremy."

"Jeremy? Pills, I think. The others? Depended on if they went to church. Beliefs and all that shit. Some just never came back to work after I told them what Pasha sees."

"What does the satellite see out there? What do you know?"

"There are universes beyond universes that no civilian knows about. As a company we've decided that it's best to not spook anyone. We found out it's better that no one knows." June could hear Canary breathing. It was a sputtering of gasps, choked off hiccups.

"What's out there?"

"Why do you want to know?"

"Just tell me. What's out there?"

"Nothing. Nothing at all."

The screen blinked and for that second of time, millions of cell phones lost service.

"We all ask, sometimes, why we're here. We get no answers so we do what we can and keep goin' on. Just moving really, right? Foot after foot of life-space until we hit the end and it's all over. I think it's really then that we get our answers so why worry about any of it now, you know?

God or whatever gave us beautiful girls to look at, to kiss, and fucking adore so let's just do that. Answers aren't gonna come any time soon unless you kill yourself this second -- which you aren't, right?"

Adulthood

WHAT you do is pull out all of the cables, the one from the computer, the printer, and the third one into the router. Count to fifteen and put them all back in."

"Why?"

"It just works that way."

All three cables went back in and all three lights lit up. Orange. Yellow. Green. This was his job, to come into offices and make things work.

The boy had the skin of yogurt. A body entirely of that light fat of an infant's inner arm. In hushed corners, he was referred to as "fetal." He was younger than me by a few years but he had his own business. We had met at an party for the opening of his competitor's new office and he gave me his card so I had called him. The router needed to work. Data needed to be shared.

In small talk he mentioned he didn't drink. The previous Sunday was spent across the bay. He had spent hours talking with his stepmother who listened to his stories of trying to meet girls, to make his way through all of those girls and find the one girl that would be his. Take her and marry her. Finish off his life with this woman and whatever children came out of her. His smile was slight but permanent. Ready to witness whatever was said with a chuckle or a click of the tongue.

"Can I get you anything? Coffee? Soda?"

"Water is fine. I don't really drink coffee or colas. They make me feel uneasy."

His body had a direct purpose. He was well trained in the maintenance of office equipment. The fat, I was sure, was just muscle at rest. Hibernating until needed. His hair was perfect and I realized I was jealous, or perhaps in love, with this boy.

"If you have any problems give me a call. Most likely from here on out any sort of problem you have can be talked through over the phone. I shouldn't have to come in."

"Right. I'll call. This is it."

"This is what?"

"The end. Our final face to face time."

"Unless something comes up. I'm happy to stop by."

I wanted to say, *"Take me with you,"* wherever he was headed, whatever world he existed in was far simpler, more pure, that the everyday I stumbled in.

By the time the train reached my apartment the air was too cold to walk the water. I made my dinner and crawled into bed. The thought of girls was pointless. The power of thought can't make a thing real. I'd have to leave my room, my apartment and hope someone found me and asked me how my day went, then I could say, "Great. Met a boy who can fix routers."

"Jesus was a horrific villain. To corral and gather a crowded mass, this is the true body of evil. The only real good is in solitude, separate mannerisms. We, mankind, are the ones that named a group of planets a universe, but earth is unto itself. Free and floating, no God above and no God below, but God within. Each of us, our own personal Lord and Savior."

Empty Hours

YOU cannot force your heart to stop beating. Instinct kicks in and the blood continues to pump. These things keep me awake at night. Playing with the control of my body. Getting tired with my eyes open. Forgetting I was still alive.

I knew a vacation would never come to me. I could plan one, even pick a destination and set off to find it, but I knew it wouldn't happen. There is too much going on that I'm built into. My name appears on too many pieces of paper and my signature is needed most days. There's something dreary about this. Staying too close to home can cause harm. Boredom. The body needs to breath a different batch of air. The mind needs to hide from new people.

In the last few years my employers have flown to Hawaii. Then Mexico. Then Portland, Oregon where I hear there are a lot of bridges but I keep seeing the same patch of the Pacific Ocean. Most days it's too cold to be at the water, but I force myself outside.

I grow restless in this city. Most nights I climb the blocks of hills to the Fairmont Hotel and pretend its white columns and curved driveway of valets are there for me. I go here and drink and if any one asks I'm from out of town. If any one were to question me, I'm on vacation. A business trip. My bags are in my room, I just needed to get a quick drink before bed. The hotel's underground tiki bar with its waterfalls and fake pond, the floating island for the band to play from, this will be my first time.

"I never knew the city had so many hills. I heard of that twisty street and the cable cars, but no one mentioned the hills."

I saw a girl past the man I spoke with. She was large with curly hair. I recognized her from a porn site I watched occasionally. She was a celebrity in the overweight adult film world. She wasn't from here but perhaps the crew was in the hotel for a shoot in one of the rooms. She was having her own faked vacation, where a man is interrupted by a busty maid who speaks perfect English.

Vodka is more expensive once inside a hotel. Call it a luxury tax. Groups of men and women in town for a wedding or a wild night in the city. Free from the reality of the office, of family and home, left in a strange place, they assume you've lost the concept of money and the quality of your free time shifts.

Each second is a new joy so I fake my own vacations, creating names and places that sound familiar, with stories that someone might believe are my own. It's only in a hotel that being nowhere in particular is a worthy reason to drink.

"We are seen as the waste of
all the empty days – us drifters,
pockets full of waded dollars
and bus transfers.

No one may like us, but they
all want to be us."

She Held My Hand and I Don't Know Why

THERE was a death to summer, when the heat waned and a draft of stiff ocean air sat on the beaches of the northern California coast. At the end of the season people still visited to run from that fear of the repeating boredom of dinner and movies, picking up the kids and paying bills. So there we were, and with us the unspoken hope that it mattered. That staring at the water was so sublime it gave meaning to itself, and in that meaning would grow our purpose.

She remembered to bring a bottle opener. The inside of my thumb was still scarred, I told her, from the last time I drank with her.

"Are we supposed to do something here?"

"I don't know. I don't think so. This might be it."

"Like take a picture, you know? Paint something. I wish I could eat this view."

"Memories only do you any good when they're the bad ones."

We drank and watched the sun set, like it always
had and always will continue to do. Her shoes
were full of sand, twin buckets of coastal earth.
She closed her eyes and leaned back against the
dune, I walked off and left her there, to maybe
find her another time. There was no point in
holding on, friendships sometimes last hours, and
some never build.

I counted the things that I could not live without and she was not one of them. At best she'd
become a memory of my former self that won't
exist in the future.
The last inch of the beer was warm and pure
foam. I tossed the bottle and heard it shatter on
the highway.

A quick thought and woosh, it was all gone.